Please Don't Litter

IDLE SPEED MANATEE ZONE

MINIMUM WAKE

D1272598

NO WAKE

Special Thanks

Dr. Emily Cullings for your valuable time and insight
during the many phases of editing.

New York Marine Rescue Center for your analysis
and experience.

To my biggest fans, Don, Sarafina, and Lucia:
I love you more than there are fish in the sea!

Dedicated to those who protect marine life all around the world. Your efforts are greatly appreciated and crucial to mankind.

—L.M.

For my amazing nieces and nephews:
Carmela, Landon, Luca, and Maddaloni.

—J.G.

www.mascotbooks.com

The Fin-Tastic Rescue

For more information, please contact:
Mascot Books
620 Herndon Parkway, Suite 320
Herndon, VA 20170
info@mascotbooks.com

Library of Congress Control Number: 2021925611

CPSIA Code: PRT0122A
ISBN-13: 978-1-63755-257-5

Printed in the United States

The Fin-Tastic Rescue

Laura Mancuso

Illustrated by Jenna Guidi

Dear Kash,

Make a splash
in this world!!

~ LK Mancuso
8/2/22

To Kash,

Dive deep into
your dreams!

[signature]

From beneath the sea on a windy autumn day,
Sara, Alix, and Lucy headed out to play.
They grabbed their sea kites and checked the tide.
Alix said, "What a perfect day for an underwater kite ride!"

The excited mermaids raced to the place
where the ocean waves break
and waited for the perfect wave, hoping to ride its wake.
Suddenly, Lucy saw a turtle out of the corner of her eye.
She tapped Sara and asked, "Hey, what's wrong with that guy?"

The concerned mermaids swam over quick.
Lucy exclaimed, "I know him! Hey, Tony, are you sick?"
Poor Tony could barely speak; he was in a daze.
"There's something wrong," said Sara as she tried to catch his gaze.

Tony was shivering and moving awfully slow.
Alix said, "I think he's *cold-stunned*; he needs a warm place to go."
Looking for answers, Lucy popped her head up out of the sea.
She said to herself, "There has to be someone who can help me."

Luckily, she spotted Beth, a friend who cleaned up the ocean.
Lucy waved her hands and made a big commotion.
Beth saw Lucy and ran to her; they were both so joyous.
Lucy called to Beth, "I'm so relieved to see you! I know you can help us!"

Lucy continued,
"You see, my friend Tony is cold and needs some assistance.
The mermaids and I can't get him home—it's too far of a distance."
Beth replied, "I will call my friends from the Marine Animal Rescue.
They have experts who will know just what to do."

Soon, Beth came on a rescue boat with a friend.
She explained, "We'll warm up Tony and put him back in the sea
when he's on the mend."
As they helped Tony onto the boat, the mermaids thanked their pal.
They all agreed that Beth was an amazing gal.

Sara began to think that when an ocean animal needed a hand, maybe Beth could help out, with the aid of her friends on land. As the mermaids arrived home to their charming underwater city, Sara turned to the girls, "I think we should start an animal rescue committee."

Alix questioned Sara, "Rescue who?"
She stared at her without a clue.
Sara responded, "Animals like Tony the turtle.
Those who can't help themselves get over a hurdle."
Lucy agreed with her sister mermaid.
"We will start in the morning and form a brigade."

The next day, they found Fifi the flamingo
with plastic wrapped around her beak.
Poor Fifi could barely eat, drink, or speak.
The mermaids called upon Beth and her Marine Rescue team.
They removed the tightly wound plastic, but Fifi was not as healthy
as it seemed.

The team decided to take Fifi to their animal hospital
for food and care.
For Fifi's sake, they also taught humans to clean up trash
and be more aware.
Fifi was released back to her home at the lagoon,
four weeks later, sometime in the afternoon.

After Fifi's welcome home celebration,
the mermaids were called to rescue another *cetacean*.
Dottie the dolphin was entangled and twisted in an old fishing net.
Lucy yelled, "She can't move. She must have a 100 pounds of line
on her, I bet!"

Alix tried to cut the lines, but Dottie was too entwined.
"It's too much. She needs to take a breath soon," she whined.
"Look who's here again!" Sara cried.
"He can help us get the lines untied!"

With the Marine Rescue's help, Dottie the dolphin was soon safe and free.
Thankfully, the team had been nearby helping a wounded manatee.
They told the mermaids how Marty the manatee
had been hit by a speeding jet ski.
Beth told them,
"*Vessel strikes* happen too often; last week there were three!"

Beth explained, "Manatees like shallow water to feed off the sea grass, but boats and jet skis come through here way too fast." She continued, "The manatees sometimes get hit by the *vessel's prop*. This harms them badly, and we need it to stop!"

Lucy said with a nod, "Humans and sea creatures need
to continue to work together.
That means facing pollution, boating laws, and bad weather."
Sara agreed, "Humans must realize they are guests in these waters.
Marine life was here first: moms, dads, sons, and daughters."

The three mermaids chorused, "Then, we can all live in harmony—every man, woman, and living being above **and** below the sea!"

Glossary

Cold-stunned: this refers to the changes sea turtles experience when they are exposed to cold water for an extended period of time. As a result of human-caused climate change, cold stunnings have become more frequent. When the water temperature drops dramatically in the fall, below fifty degrees, it becomes a threat to turtles. Turtles are reptiles that rely on an external heat source to warm up their bodies. When a turtle becomes cold-stunned, they are not able to eat, swim, or warm up in frigid waters. This leads to a slower heart rate, frostbite, pneumonia, and quite possibly death.

(Turtle Restoration Network: seaturtles.org)

Cetacean: [si-tay-shn] a marine mammal of the order Cetacea; a large aquatic mammal such as a whale, dolphin, or porpoise (*Merriam-Webster*)

Vessel: a ship or boat

Prop: a boat propeller

Vessel Strike: a collision between any type of boat and a marine mammal in the ocean. All sizes and types of vessels, from large ships to jet skis, have the potential to collide with any marine species. (fisheries.noaa.gov)

Sea Turtle Species
Green Sea Turtle

- Green turtles are not named for the color of their shell, which is normally brown or olive, but for the green color of their skin.

- Unlike most sea turtles, adult green turtles lean towards the diet of an herbivore and feed on sea grasses and algae. However, juvenile green turtles have been known to feed on invertebrates like crabs, jellyfish, and sponges.

- Green sea turtles are also known for warming themselves by sunbathing on beaches, just like seals and albatrosses. This species is one of the only sea turtle species to leave the water other than to lay eggs.

Sources: worldwildlife.org; nymarinerescue.org

Loggerhead

- Loggerhead turtles are named for their large heads and powerful jaw muscles. Their jaws allow them to feed on hard shellfish and sea urchins.

- A loggerhead female will lay her eggs at the beach where she was hatched, sometimes traveling thousands of miles to get there. They lay their eggs under the sand on these beaches, which are often frequented by humans. Due to human interference, the eggs need protection and care to prevent them from being destroyed.

- Loggerheads have played a crucial part of our marine ecosystem for over 100 million years, keeping coral reefs and sea grass beds healthy.

Sources: worldwildlife.org; nationalgeographic.com

Leatherback

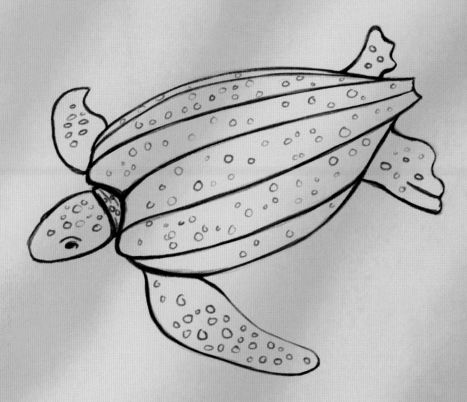

- Leatherbacks get their name from their shell, which is leather-like and rubbery, rather than hard like other turtles. They have existed in this form since the age of the dinosaurs.

- Leatherbacks are the largest of all the sea turtle species. They can weigh up to 1,300 pounds and grow to be as big as six feet. They are the fourth largest reptile in the world.

- Unlike other reptiles, leatherbacks have been known to inhabit waters with temperatures ranging from zero to fifteen degrees Celsius. This suggests they are capable of thermoregulation (controlling their internal body temperature).

Sources: noaa.org; nymarinerescue.org

Kemp's ridley

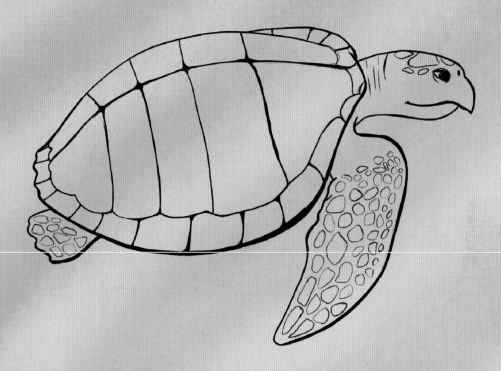

- Also known as the Atlantic ridley, the Kemp's ridley is the most endangered species of all sea turtles.

- They prefer shallow waters, where they can dive to the bottom to feed on crabs, their favorite food. The Kemp's ridley also feeds on shellfish, jellyfish, seaweed, and sargassum.

- Kemp's ridleys can live up to thirty years in the wild.

Sources: nationalgeographic.com; nymarinerescue.org

Flamingo

- Flamingos are a type of wading bird that live in large shallow lakes, lagoons, mangrove swamps, tidal flats, and sandy islands.

- They are born white or gray and turn pink from carotenoids, a type of pigment found in their diet of brine shrimp, snails, blue-green algae, and plankton.

- When a flamingo eats, it plunges its head underwater and twists its neck so it is upside down. Then, it scoops up the food, using its upper beak like a shovel.

- Flamingos are very social animals and live in a group called a flamboyance.

- They are famously known for standing on one leg. Although scientists do not completely understand why, some think it is to conserve body heat.

Sources: sciencekids.co.nz; nationalgeographickids.com; coolkidsfacts.com

Manatee

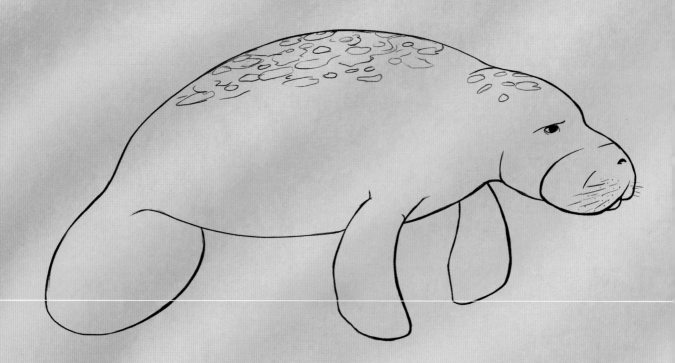

- Manatees are mammals of substantial size. Despite their size, they are graceful swimmers who use their powerful tails to propel them through the water at an average of five mph.

- Manatees grow to be eight to thirteen feet long and weigh in at 440 lbs. to 1,300 lbs.

- Manatees are nicknamed sea cows.

- Manatees are vegetarians, feeding on large amounts of water grasses, weeds, and algae. They can eat a tenth of their weight in twenty-four hours.

- These gentle giants are often accidentally hit by motorboats or entangled in fishing nets in increasingly crowded waters.

Source: nationalgeographic.com

Dolphin

- There are thirty-six species of dolphins that inhabit our oceans.

- Most dolphins are marine mammals, although there are a few species that live in freshwater rivers and streams.

- Dolphins feed mostly on fish and squid and use a built-in sonar system called echolocation to find their prey.

- Atlantic Spotted Dolphins are described as "acrobatic" swimmers, frequently leaping out of the water. They swim very quickly and are known to surf in the waves created by vessels.

- Atlantic Spotted Dolphins are not born with their spots; they develop them after about three years.

Sources: nationalgeographic.com; fisheries.noaa.gov

About the Author

Laura Mancuso grew up loving the beach and marine biology in St. James, New York. After graduating from the University of Buffalo, she continued to live and work in Buffalo, New York, with her husband. However, she missed her family and friends—and the ocean, too! Laura made her way back home to Long Island. Inspired by her daughters' love of mermaids and nature, Laura decided to start writing children's books. With her writing, she hopes to encourage young children to love reading while drawing awareness to the preservation of our waters. Laura currently lives in Hampton Bays, where you can find her with her family at one of its many beautiful beaches.

The Fin-Tastic Rescue is Laura's second children's book, following 2021's *The Fin-Tastic Cleanup.*

Learn more at laura-mancuso.com.

About the Illustrator

Jenna Guidi grew up on Long Island and studied illustration and animation at the School of Visual Arts in New York City. Jenna's work has been featured in Netflix shows, and this is the second children's book she has illustrated. Since Jenna was a little girl, she has loved Disney and Pixar films, which sparked her lifelong interest in art. When she is not drawing, she is usually reading, baking, and drinking tea. Traveling has given her a greater appreciation of the earth, and she believes we must do the best we can to take care of our planet and each other.

For more information visit jennaguidi.com.

DO NOT FEED WILDLIFE

WATCH FOR WILDLIFE

Conservation Area

Ground Nesting Birds

WE ARE BITTER ABOUT LITTER

WASH THE WAVES

Please Don't Litter

IDLE SPEED

MANATEE ZONE

MINIMUM WAKE

NO

WAKE

DO NOT FEED WILDLIFE

WATCH FOR WILDLIFE

Conservation Area

Ground Nesting Birds

WE ARE BITTER ABOUT LITTER

WASH THE WAVES